JUST BIG ENOUGH

 A Big Tuna Trading Company, LLC/J. R. Sansevere Book

www.harperchildrens.com
www.littlecritter.com

Library of Congress Cataloging-in-Publication Data is available from the publisher.

1 2 3 4 5 6 7 8 9 10
❖
First Edition

JUST BIG ENOUGH

BY MERCER MAYER

HarperFestival®

A Division of HarperCollinsPublishers

Every morning on my way to school, I always sit in the same seat on the school bus. But this morning . . .

. . . a big kid took my seat.

"Excuse me," I said. "You're sitting in my seat."
The big kid didn't move. I guess he didn't hear me.

At recess, I wanted to play football with the big kids, but they said I couldn't play because I was too small.

And at lunch, the big kids took all of the cupcakes.
They laughed when I said they had to share. They told
me the cupcakes were just for them.

"I wish I were bigger," I said to my friends.
They nodded.
"I bet there are lots of ways to grow," I said.

After school, my mom measured me.

"How can I make myself grow?" I asked Mom.

"Eat your vegetables," she said. "They will make you big and strong."

So at dinner, I ate almost all my spinach and a whole bunch of carrots.

"Am I bigger yet?" I asked Mom.

"Not yet," said Mom.

Later, I asked Dad what would make me grow.
"Exercise," he said.

So, I did jumping
jacks . . .

sit-ups . . .

. . . and push-ups
. . . and I ran around and
around.

After all that exercise
I didn't get any bigger,
but I sure got tired.

That night, I couldn't sleep. So, I read a comic book.
And that's when I got a great idea.

The next morning, I asked Dad for some wood and some glue. Mom gave me tinfoil. And Little Sister let me have a jar of her glitter.

"What are you making?" asked Little Sister.

"A growing machine," I said.

I worked on the growing machine all morning. When it was finished, I sprinkled glitter on it so it sparkled like the one in the comic book I had read.

I made a helmet out of tinfoil.

Then I put on my helmet and climbed into the growing machine.

I sat in the growing machine
all afternoon.

I even ate my lunch there.

When it became dark, Dad said it was time to come home.

"Did I grow?" I asked.

Dad shook his head and said, "Not yet."

"Maybe I should sleep in the growing machine," I said.
Dad didn't think that was such a good idea.

The next day, I went to Grandma and Grandpa's farm.

"What's the matter, Little Critter?" asked Grandpa.
I told Grandpa about the big kids and how I was trying to get big, too, so that I could do all the things the big kids did.

Grandpa took me out to the meadow.
"Look at those two horses," he said.
"Which one do you think is the fastest?"
"The big one!" I said.

Grandpa let the big horse and the little horse loose.
They started to run across the field.

And do you know which one was the fastest?
The little one.

The next day at school, the big kids said again that I couldn't play football because I was too small. I started to get mad.

"I challenge you to a relay race," I said. "The big kids against the little kids."

The big kids laughed, but they said okay.

The whole school came to watch the race.

And you know what?

The little kids won!

So, I guess sometimes being small is
just big enough.